Sleep Tight

By Constance Allen
Illustrated by David Prebenna

Dalmatian Press, LLC, 2009. All rights reserved.
Published by Dalmatian Press, LLC, 2009. The DALMATIAN PRESS name and logo are trademarks of Dalmatian Press, LLC, Franklin, Tennessee 37067. No part of this book may be reproduced or copied in any form without written permission from the copyright owner.

Printed in the U.S.A.

11 12 13 B&M 37631 10 9 8 7
15302 Sesame Street 8x8 Storybook: Sleep Tight!

"Time to go home, Elmo!" calls Elmo's daddy.
"Just one more game of monster tag, please,
Daddy?" asks Elmo.
"Okay. One more game," says Elmo's daddy.

On the way home from the park, Elmo
and his daddy see lots of other people
on their way home, too.
It's almost bedtime for little monsters.

On Sesame Street, everyone is getting ready for bed.

Splish, splash! Little Bird shakes his feathers in his warm bath.

Sleepy monsters comb their fur
and brush their teeth.

Flossie isn't sleepy yet. Herry and Flossie do stretches.

"… Seven, eight, nine, ten," pants Herry Monster. "Are you getting sleepy, Flossie?"

Flossie shakes her head.

"Ten slow toe touches," says Herry. "One… two… three… four…"

Oscar finishes his book, *Mother Grouch Rhymes*.
  "Little Boy Grouch, come blow your kazoo.
  Take a mud bath and eat anchovy stew..."
He closes his book.
Sleep tight, sleepy grouch.

Big Bird sings his teddy bear a lullaby.
"Rock-a-bye, Radar, snug in my nest.
Time for us both to lie down and rest!
Sleep tight, little bear," says Big Bird.

At the Snuffleupagus cave, it's bedtime for Alice.
Boing! Boing! Boing!
She bounces on the bed.
Sleep tight, Alice.

In the Count's castle, the Count counts sheep.
"One sheep! Two sheep! Three beautiful wool-
ly sheep!" cries the Count.
Sleep tight, Count.

In the country, Cowboy Grover settles down to sleep under the stars.
"Sleep tight, little cows!" he calls.

In the city, Hoots the Owl plays a saxophone serenade above the city lights.
Bee-boop-a-diddly-diddly-doo-wha-doo!
"I'll keep things cool till morning," he croons. "Sleep tight, everyone."

In Ernie's window box, sleepy Twiddlebugs
snuggle under their leaf blankets.
Sleep tight, little Twiddlebugs.

All is quiet on Sesame Street. Monsters and birds and grouches and Twiddlebugs sleep soundly in their beds.

Sleep tight, little Elmo.